EGMONT
We bring stories to life

First published in Great Britain 2008 by Egmont UK Limited
239 Kensington High Street, London W8 6SA
LazyTown © & TM 2008 LazyTown Entertainment.
All related titles, logos and characters are trademarks
of LazyTown Entertainment.
© 2008 LazyTown Entertainment. All rights reserved.

ISBN 978 1 4052 3760 4

1 3 5 7 9 10 8 6 4 2

Printed in Malaysia

# The Lazy Genie

**"K**eep LazyTown lazy! That's the Robbie Rotten way! Let me tell you what happened when I met a genie who could grant my wishes and maybe even get rid of that Sportacus once and for all! I really don't like that Sportaloon . . .**"**

*As you read this story, there are games and activities along the way. Why not give them a try? Then you can be more like Sportacus and his friends – they love to keep their minds and bodies active, unlike Robbie Rotten!*

**O**n a sunny day in LazyTown, Ziggy and his friends met at the vegetable patch to plant and water their seeds. But somebody was missing.

"No sign of Stingy yet?" asked Stephanie. "Maybe he forgot!"

"I'll go look for him," Ziggy volunteered.

But Stingy was too busy to help plant vegetables. He was behaving very strangely indeed, standing in the Town Square with his eyes closed!

"Wishing, wishing, wishing . . . " he muttered, but he was interrupted when Robbie bumped into him.

"Out of my way, Sticky!" Robbie grumbled.

"I can't move," Stingy told him, "I'm wishing for money!"

Robbie thought for a moment. "Does that work?" Then he realised how silly Stingy was being. "Of course it doesn't work!"

Robbie shook his head, and sneaked away.

Next, Ziggy arrived in the Town Square to find Stingy wishing.

"Oh, there you are, Stingy," said Ziggy. "You said that you were going to help us plant the vegetables."

Stingy waved him away. "Shhh! Wishing, wishing! Oh, I'm wishing with all my might . . . "

Suddenly Stingy reached into his pocket and pulled out a coin.

**"It worked!"** he exclaimed. *"I wished for a coin and here it is!"*

Robbie, who had been watching the whole time, was amazed. "Wishes come true? Why didn't anyone tell me that?" he squawked, and ran away.

Ziggy decided that Stingy should tell Stephanie what had happened.

But Stephanie wasn't convinced that Stingy's wish had come true. "Stingy always has coins in his pocket," she reminded Ziggy. "You can't just wish for things, you have to work for them."

7

**M**eanwhile, Robbie had had an idea. If his own wishes wouldn't come true, he would find somebody to grant wishes for him! And who better than a genie?

As if by magic, a lamp dropped into Robbie's lap. He rubbed it with a rag and suddenly –

# KABLOOM!

Out popped a
very large genie!

"I am the Grand Genie of
Eternity!" he boomed.
"The greatest genie of the centuries!"

Robbie looked the genie up and down.
"How do I know that you are a real
genie?" he challenged.

With a click of his fingers, the genie proved himself by floating above LazyTown on his magic carpet.

"**I** wanna wish! I wanna wish!" Robbie demanded. But the genie would only grant a wish if Robbie gave him some cake. No wonder he was such a large genie!

Robbie kept pestering the genie. "I'll give you all the cake you want if you give me three wishes."

The genie asked Robbie for his first wish.

"To get rid of all the fruits and vegetables in LazyTown," Robbie declared.

**"No problemo,"** the genie boomed and cast his spell . . .

Back at the vegetable patch, Stingy was sure he could prove to his friends that wishing did work!

But Stephanie and Ziggy were more interested in growing their vegetables. Stingy was very annoyed! Why didn't his friends believe him?

"I just wish all the fruit and vegetables would disappear!" he huffed.

In a flash of sparkling light, Stephanie's and Ziggy's vegetables disappeared!

"Stingy, how did you do that?" Stephanie gasped, staring at the now empty vegetable patch.

**"T**hose disgusting vegetables!" Robbie cackled, delighted that they had all gone . . . but where was the genie?

He had disappeared back into his lamp! "Where are my wishes?" Robbie demanded, tapping on the lamp. "My next wish is that you get rid of all the sports equipment in LazyTown."

But first, Robbie had to show the genie what sports equipment was. He tried to teach the genie to play basketball, but the genie was much better at the game than Robbie was!

"Stop playing!" Robbie sulked. "You were supposed to get rid of that stuff, not play with it! I wish that you'd get rid of all the sports equipment!"

The genie began to cast his second spell . . .

**A**t the very same time, Stephanie and Ziggy were chasing after Stingy, begging him to reverse his wish and bring the vegetables back.

"Quit picking on me!" Stingy grumbled. "It's not like I wished for all the sports equipment to disappear!"

# Uh-oh!

In a flash of sparkling light, all the nets, balls, hoops and bats disappeared from the sports field.

High in his airship, Sportacus's crystal began to beep. His friends were in trouble!

"**All** the fruits and vegetables are gone," Robbie cackled in delight. "All the sports equipment is gone. And it's gone FOREVER!"

The genie frowned at Robbie. "You didn't say anything about forever," he said slowly.

Robbie started to panic! "So the stuff isn't gone forever?" he shrieked. "When is it coming back?"

The genie shrugged and said, "Right about . . . now!"

Meanwhile, Stingy had had enough of his wishes coming true – they were all going wrong! His friends were annoyed with him, there were no fruits or vegetables in LazyTown and nothing to play with!

"Oh, I wish everything was just the way it was," he sighed.

# WHOOSH!

The sports equipment reappeared on the field. In the vegetable patch, the vegetables reappeared and the fruits returned to the trees all over LazyTown!

**"You did it!"** Stephanie gasped.

**"H**i guys, what's the trouble?"** Sportacus asked his friends as he landed. LazyTown seemed perfectly normal to him. Ziggy told him everything that had happened, and Stingy assured him that everything was fine now.

All the same, Sportacus decided to look around and make sure . . .

Robbie remembered he had one more wish. "I want Sportacus out of LazyTown forever," he told the genie.

"Who's Sportacus?" the genie asked – just as the superhero appeared in front of them!

Robbie pointed wildly. **"He's that guy!"**

The genie began to grant Robbie's wish – but Sportacus was too fast for him to catch!

Sportacus flipped and zipped, ducked and dived, and wore out the lazy genie very quickly!

**"D**id you get him? Is he gone?" Robbie asked the genie excitedly.

"I couldn't . . . catch him," the genie panted. Angry Robbie began to stamp and sulk, growl and grunt.

"You said you were the best genie in the world!" Robbie grumbled. "If you make one more mistake," he shrieked shrilly as he shook the lamp, "I will throw this away and you won't have a home any more!"

"OK, OK," huffed the puffed-out genie. "But how are we going to catch that blue blur?

**He's too fast!"**

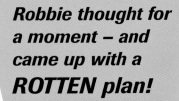

*Robbie thought for a moment – and came up with a ROTTEN plan!*

*R*obbie rummaged behind his bench, where he sometimes hid his tools. With a grunt, he pulled out the heaviest one – an iron anvil!

Robbie lifted the anvil with difficulty and dropped it on the end of the seesaw. Then he found a big, white letter X in his pile of odd things. "This goes here," he told the genie, throwing the X on the ground near the seesaw. "When Sportaloon lands on the X, I'll jump on to the seesaw, then the anvil will fly up and land on him!"

The genie liked the sound of Robbie's rotten plan. "And then . . . I zippety-whippety him away!" he cackled gleefully.

Robbie looked around. "He's coming," he announced, spotting Sportacus flipping towards them.

"Get ready . . . "

23

**C**lutching the lamp under his arm, Robbie climbed onto the wall to wait for Sportacus, as the genie hid behind the bench.

"Here he comes!" Robbie hissed in delight. The plan was about to come into action!

Sportacus leaped over the wall and landed on the top end of the seesaw, sending the anvil flying through the air, then ran straight over the X in a flash of blue.

"What?!" Robbie ran over to see what had happened – and peered down. He was standing right on top of the X – and the anvil was plummeting towards his head!

Robbie gave a startled scream. The genie shouted,

## "Disappear!"

just in the nick of time, as the anvil came crashing to the ground, smack-bang on top of the X!

"That wasn't supposed to happen," muttered the genie. Suddenly, his lamp came hurtling through the sky towards the hard ground. "My home!" he wailed.

**A**s Sportacus fled the sports field, his crystal began to beep again. "Someone's in trouble!" he realised, and zipped right back to where the genie stood, too shocked to move, as his lamp fell through the sky.

Sportacus threw himself down on the ground, and caught the lamp just in time! "Got it!" he laughed, very relieved.

"You saved my home!" the genie exclaimed in amazement as Sportacus gave him back the lamp. "Thank you!"

**T**he kids rushed over to see what had happened and stopped abruptly when they saw Sportacus's new friend.

"It's a genie!" Stingy exclaimed.

"Duh, genius!" Ziggy laughed.

"Are you a real genie?" asked Stingy, a little doubtfully.

"I am the Grand Genie of All Ages, the greatest genie of the centuries," the genie boomed.

Suddenly Stingy realised what had been happening that day! "So, it was you who made the sports equipment and vegetables disappear!" he said, very pleased with himself.

"Sorry about that," the genie said sheepishly. "I was also trying to get rid of you," he admitted to Sportacus. "But instead I got rid of that skinny dude in the stripy suit. Forever."

28

**L**ooking at the friends' horrified faces, the genie realised he'd made a mistake. He cleared his throat quickly. "Since you saved my home, I'll grant you one special wish!" he told Sportacus. But Sportacus decided to give his wish to Stingy – who did enjoy wishing, after all!

Stingy thought hard. "Well . . . it's not LazyTown without vegetables, and it's not LazyTown without sports equipment, and it's not LazyTown without you, Sportacus!"

Stingy's friends nodded in agreement.

" . . . and it's not LazyTown without the skinny dude in the stripy suit!" Stingy gasped. "I wish for him to be returned!"

The genie cast his spell – and Robbie fell from the sky!

"I wish . . . " Robbie was spluttering as he struggled to his feet.

"No more wishes for you!" the genie interrupted Robbie. "But I have one more wish for myself before I go home."

"Really? What's that?" Sportacus asked.

# "Let's dance!"
the genie boomed.

Everyone joined in and danced, pleased that everything was back to normal in LazyTown – even Robbie!

# Genie, Genie, Grant My Wish!

Why not play **Genie, Genie, Grant My Wish**?
Players take turns to ask another player, the genie, to grant them a wish to help them reach the finish line. But the genie might not always want to grant a wish!

## Go find . . .

2+ friends to play with
2 objects to mark the start line and the finish line

## Go play!

Use one object to mark the start line and one to mark the finish line, 20 paces apart.

Next, choose a friend to play the genie. The genie should stand behind the finish line, while his friends stand behind the start line, facing him.

Players take turns to ask the genie permission to move forward to the finish line. Each player must begin their question, "Genie, Genie, Grant My Wish. May I . . . " and ask to move forward in any one of three ways.

Players must not take more than three steps in one turn.

**1** Take *1/2/3* steps forward

**2** Hop *1/2/3* times forward

**3** Skip *1/2/3* times forward

**4** Jump *1/2/3* times forward

The genie has three choices for answering:

**1 "Yes, your wish is granted!"** The player can move as they choose.

**2 "No, your wish is denied, but you may . . . "** The player cannot move as they choose but the genie can choose a different way, for instance, "you may take one step sideways!" The genie can also tell a player to move backwards if he wishes.

**3 "No, your wish is denied!"** The player cannot move at all in that turn!

If a player forgets to say, **"Genie, Genie, Grant My Wish"**, before asking the genie's permission to move, the genie's answer is always, "No, your wish is denied!" That player must return to the start line.

The winner is the first player to reach the finish line – he or she then becomes the genie and the game begins again!

# Guessing Games

Why not play **Guessing Games**? This game is like **Charades** but players mime different sports with as much movement, action and energy as they can. Their friends must guess what they are playing!

When Robbie's wish makes the sports equipment disappear, there's nothing for the LazyTown kids to play with! How will they get active now?

## Go find...

2+ friends
A coin

## Go play!

Toss the coin to see who begins the game of **Guessing Games** – they become the Acting Athlete.

The Acting Athlete must think of a sport and mime it for everyone else, who must call out what sport he or she is playing.

For example, if the Acting Athlete is pretending to hold reins and gallop, players could guess, **"Ice skating!"**, **"Gymnastics!"** and finally **"Horse-racing!"**

The first player who guesses correctly joins in with the Acting Athlete and the two players continue miming until other players call out, **"Game over!"**

The player who guessed correctly then becomes the Acting Athlete and thinks of a new sport to mime.

*"I can do it!"*

35

# Skip the X

*Robbie tries to help the genie to catch Sportacus by tricking him into landing on the letter X!*

**Skip the X** is based on French Skipping, using elastic – but you must be careful not to land on the X by accident!

## Go find . . .

2 friends

A long piece of elastic, tied into a loop (ask an adult to cut and tie this for you)

## Go play!

Choose two friends to hold the elastic – Friend 1 and Friend 2. They should stand about 1 metre apart, facing each other, with their feet quite wide apart.

Place the elastic behind Friend 1's ankles, then hold it out and twist it over once, before placing the other end of the loop behind Friend 2's ankles. You should now see an **X** between your friends' feet!

Skip over the X but do not touch the elastic. If you do, you must swap places with Friend 1 or 2. Why not try . . .

# I Love LazyTown?

Jump into each of the 4 segments of the X as you chant the rhyme and turn in each direction. Start in section 1:

**"North** or **South,** *[2],* **East,** *[3]* or **West** *[4],* **Where** *[1]* **in the world** *[section 2]* **do I like it** *[3]* **BEST?** *[4]"*

The answer is *LazyTown* of course!

# Jumpin' Genie

Jump into two sections of the X at a time. You need energy for this rhyme! Start with your feet in sections 1 and 2. As you chant the rhyme, jump to your right each time to move into two different sections until you've turned a full circle!

**"Genie, Genie,"** *[jump into sections 3 and 4]*

**"Cake on a dish,"** *[sections 2 and 1]*

**"How many times"** *[jump into sections 4 and 3]*

**"Can you grant a wish?"** *[jump into sections 1 and 2 again]*

Now jump into each section in turn, until you can jump no longer!

*"Go for it!"*

# Memory Games

Why not play some memory games?

Can you remember . . .

## Who . . .

**1**. . . went to find Stingy when he didn't meet his friends at the vegetable patch?

**2**. . . caught the genie's lamp before it fell to the ground?

**3**. . . did Sportacus give his wish to?

## What . . .

**1**. . . did Stingy first wish for?

**2** . . . game did Robbie teach the genie to play?

**3** . . . did Robbie place on the seesaw to catch Sportacus?

?

38

# Where...

... do these objects belong?

Can you find each one on a different page?

**1**

**2**

**3**

# Look Closely . . .

There are **5** magic lamps hidden in this picture.

*Can you find them all?*